19

TRIANGLE HISTORIES
★ ★ ★ ★ ★ ★ ★
THE CIVIL WAR

THE BATTLE OF
BULL RUN

Deborah Kops

BLACKBIRCH PRESS, INC.

WOODBRIDGE, CONNECTICUT

For Noah

Published by Blackbirch Press, Inc.
260 Amity Road
Woodbridge, CT 06525

Web site: http://www.blackbirch.com
e-mail: staff@blackbirch.com

Printed in China

10 9 8 7 6 5 4 3 2 1

Photo credits:
Cover, back cover, pages 7 (inset), 20, 21, 26 (left), 24, 28, 29, 30: North Wind Picture Archives; pages 7, 8, 14, 15, 17, 18, 25, 27: Library of Congress; pages 11, 19, 22 (right), 23: National Archives.

Library of Congress Cataloging-in-Publication Data
Kops, Deborah.
The Battle of Bull Run / by Deborah Kops.
        p. cm. — (The Civil War)
Summary: Presents the events leading up to the first major battle in the Civil War, at Bull Run in 1861, and describes that clash and its aftermath.
Includes index.
        ISBN 1-56711-553-5 (hardcover: alk. paper)
1. Bull Run, 1st Battle of, Va., 1861—Juvenile literature. [1. Bull Run, 1st Battle of, Va., 1861. 2. United States—History—Civil War, 1861–1865—Campaigns.]
I. Title. II. Civil War (Blackbirch Press)
E472.18.K67 2001
973.7'31—dc21   2001002570

CONTENTS

Preface: The Civil War.. 4

Introduction:
  A Picnic on a Summer Day 6

Closing in on Manassas.. 8

McDowell Lays Out Plans.. 9

Beauregard Plans His Strategy........................ 11

McDowell's March to Bull Run...................... 12

McDowell Refines His Strategy..................... 14

McDowell's Early Morning Attack................. 16

"Standing Like a Stone Wall".......................... 21

The Federals Run.. 25

After Bull Run.. 27

Glossary.. 31

For More Information.. 31

Index.. 32

PREFACE: THE CIVIL WAR

Nearly 150 years after the final shots were fired, the Civil War remains one of the key events in U. S. history. The enormous loss of life alone makes it tragically unique: More Americans died in Civil War battles than in all other American wars combined. More Americans fell at the Battle of Gettysburg than during any battle in American military history. And, in one day at the Battle of Antietam, more Americans were killed and wounded than in any other day in American history.

As tragic as the loss of life was, however, it is the principles over which the war was fought that make it uniquely American. Those beliefs—equality and freedom—are the foundation of American democracy, our basic rights. It was the bitter disagreement about the exact nature of those rights that drove our nation to its bloodiest war.

The disagreements grew in part from the differing economies of the North and South. The warm climate and wide-open areas of the Southern states were ideal for an economy based on agriculture. In the first half of the 19th century, the main cash crop was cotton, grown on large farms called plantations. Slaves, who were brought to the United States from Africa, were forced to do the backbreaking work of planting and harvesting cotton. They also provided the other labor necessary to keep plantations running. Slaves were bought and sold like property, and had been critical to the Southern economy since the first Africans came to America in 1619.

The suffering of African Americans under slavery is one of the great tragedies in American history. And the debate over whether the United States government had the right to forbid slavery—in both Southern states and in new territories—was a dispute that overshadowed the first 80 years of our history.

For many Northerners, the question of slavery was one of morality and not economics. Because the Northern economy was based on manufacturing rather than agriculture, there was little need for slave labor. The primary economic need of Northern states was a protective tax known as a tariff that would make imported goods more expensive than goods made in the North. Tariffs forced Southerners to buy Northern goods and made them economically dependent on the North, a fact that led to deep resentment among Southerners.

Economic control did not matter to the anti-slavery Northerners known as abolitionists. Their conflict with the South was over slavery. The idea that the federal government could outlaw slavery was perfectly reasonable. After all, abolitionists contended, our nation was founded on the idea that all people are created equal. How could slavery exist in such a country?

For the Southern states that joined the Confederacy, the freedom from unfair taxation and the right to make their own decisions about slavery was as important a principle as equality. For most Southerners, the right of states to decide what is best for its citizens was the most important principle guaranteed in the Constitution.

The conflict over these principles generated sparks throughout the decades leading up to the Civil War. The importance of keeping an equal number of slave and free states in the Union became critical to Southern lawmakers in Congress in those years. In 1820, when Maine and Missouri sought admission to the Union, the question was settled by the Missouri Compromise: Maine was admitted as a free state, Missouri as a slave state, thus maintaining a balance in Congress. The compromise stated that all future territories north of the southern boundary of Missouri would enter the Union as free states, those south of it would be slave states.

In 1854, however, the Kansas-Nebraska Act set the stage for the Civil War. That act repealed the Missouri Compromise and, by declaring that the question of slavery should be decided by residents of the territory, set off a rush of pro- and anti-slavery settlers to the new land. Violence between the two sides began almost immediately and soon "Bleeding Kansas" became a tragic chapter in our nation's story.

With Lincoln's election on an anti-slavery platform in 1860, the disagreement over the power of the federal government reached its breaking point. South Carolina became the first state to secede from the Union, followed by Mississippi, Florida, Alabama, Georgia, Louisiana, Virginia, Texas, North Carolina, Tennessee, and Arkansas. Those eleven states became the Confederate States of America. Confederate troops fired the first shots of the Civil War at Fort Sumter, South Carolina, on April 12, 1861. Those shots began a four-year war in which thousands of Americans—Northerners and Southerners—would give, in President Lincoln's words, "the last full measure of devotion."

INTRODUCTION:
A PICNIC ON A SUMMER DAY

★ ★ ★ ★ ★

On the warm summer weekend of July 20 and 21, 1861, a large gathering of Union supporters—congressmen, senators, and wealthy gentlemen and ladies from Washington, D.C.—left the nation's capital in a long parade of horses and buggies. They were headed toward the small town of Manassas Junction about thirty miles west of the city. Many in the enormous throng planned to enjoy a picnic as they witnessed the first battle of the Civil War.

The conflict was a little more than three months old, and most in the assembly believed that this would be the one large battle that would bring an end to what some were confidently calling "the six month war." They expected a Union victory at Manassas would be followed by the fall of Richmond, Virginia, the Confederate capital. Many spectators planned to be back in the capital by late Sunday. By then, most agreed, the Rebels would be on the run.

In Manassas, near the Bull Run River, about 20,000 Confederates waited impatiently, cleaning their weapons and making last-minute battle preparations. They knew nothing of the picnickers heading their way. Their attention was focused on the Union troops.

The Union soldiers were camped about six miles from Manassas, enjoying the parade of onlookers arriving from Washington. A young man from Connecticut called out, "There's our senator!" A soldier from Massachusetts later remembered, "We thought it wasn't a bad idea to have the great men from Washington come out to see us thrash the Rebs."

No one among them could have known that the picnic would end in smoke, screams of dying men, and a panicked retreat. And no one on either side could possibly have imagined that the Battle of Bull Run would be just the first in a four-year war that ripped our nation apart.

OPPOSITE PAGE: Bull Run River
INSET: Union supporters packed picnics to watch the battle of Bull Run.

CLOSING IN ON MANASSAS

In 1861, at the beginning of the Civil War, neither side believed that full-scale battles or major invasions would be necessary to end the conflict. Confederate President Jefferson Davis favored the same strategy used by George Washington against the British. He planned to wear down the North's desire to continue the war by fighting defensive battles, attacking isolated military bases, and retreating when necessary.

On the Union side, seventy-four-year-old General Winfield Scott, commander of the Union army, followed the principles of warfare that had been accepted for centuries—cut off supplies to enemy forces and capture its capital. As part of this strategy, Scott created what became known as the "Anaconda Plan," named after the large snake that killed by wrapping its body around its prey and crushing it.

Jefferson Davis,
President of
The Confederate
States of America

Scott's plan called for cutting off the South from foreign aid by blockading its port cities along the coast and sending a fleet of gunboats down the Mississippi River. This would cut Southern supply lines and split the Confederacy at the Mississippi.

As confident as both leaders were in their plans, Davis and Scott were forced to change by an impatient public eager for military action. Southerners clamored for a march against Washington, D.C. For their part, many Northerners demanded an invasion, beginning at Manassas, where about 20,000 Confederates were assembled under General P.T. Beauregard, commander of the forces that took Fort Sumter. From there, the Union forces would continue to Richmond, Virginia, the Confederate capital, where the Southern congress was scheduled to meet in July 1861.

The New York *Herald Tribune,* one of the most widely read newspapers of the time, helped fan the Union fires with its headline:

FORWARD TO RICHMOND! FORWARD TO RICHMOND!
The Rebel Congress Must Not Be Allowed to Meet There on the 20th of July!

What's the Name of That Battle?

The Confederates and the Federals gave different names to a number of Civil War battles. Southerners named most battles after the towns in which they were fought, while the Union named them after a landmark near the fighting—often a river or stream. The Battle of Bull Run, for example, is the name used by Northerners who named it for the river that ran through the battlefield. That same battle was called Manassas in the South. Antietam, named for Antietam Creek, was called the battle of Sharpsburg by the Confederates. The opposite case is the battle of Shiloh, named by rebels after the church near the spot where they launched an attack. Among Union supporters, the battle was known for its location, Pittsburg Landing.

President Lincoln was among the many people who believed that a successful attack on the 20,000 Confederates gathered under Beauregard would lead to the capture of Richmond, about eighty miles south of Manassas. Eager to put an end to the war as quickly as possible, he ordered the Union force to plan an attack.

McDowell Lays Out Plans

In early June 1861, General Scott asked General Irvin McDowell, commander of the Union troops in Washington, D.C., to develop a

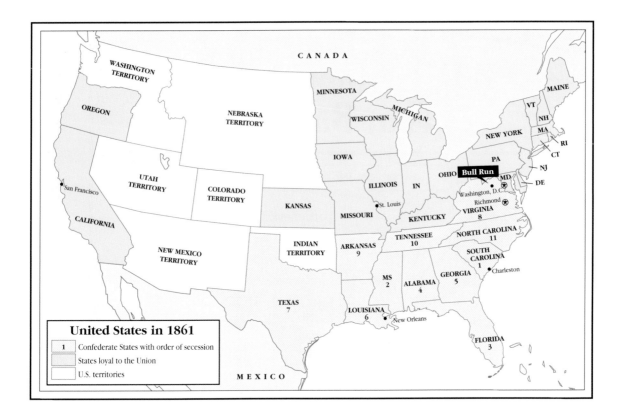

Map caption/legend:

United States in 1861

1	Confederate States with order of secession
	States loyal to the Union
	U.S. territories

plan for an advance on Manassas. McDowell had been an officer under Scott, as well as a classmate of Beauregard's at the United States Military Academy at West Point, New York. McDowell had no experience as a commander on a battlefield, however, he was well trained in military strategy. A key part of his plan called for a flank, or side, attack on the Confederate forces in Manassas.

McDowell developed his plan knowing that about 11,000 Confederates were stationed at the federal arsenal in nearby Harpers Ferry, which they had taken over in April just after the war had broken out. Positioned between Harpers Ferry and Manassas were 15,000 Union men under the command of Major General Robert Patterson, a sixty-nine-year-old veteran of the War of 1812. McDowell knew that, for his plan to succeed, it was essential for Patterson's force to prevent the Confederates from reinforcing Beauregard's 20,000-man fighting corps in Manassas.

Beauregard Plans His Strategy

In the Confederate camp, Beauregard knew that McDowell would march on Manassas, but he didn't know exactly when. While he waited, he organized his troops and drew up his own defensive plan. He divided his brigade into six regiments, placing three at the three main approaches to Manassas from Washington, D.C., and the remaining three close around Manassas itself.

Confederate Brigadier General Milledge L. Bonham.

Confederate Brigadier General Milledge L. Bonham, whose regiment was stationed at a crossroads closest to Washington, D.C., ordered his men to cut down trees over the road to slow down the Federals. Elsewhere, General Richard Ewell and his men were positioned five miles south of Bonham on another road. Brigadier General Philip St. George Cocke and his Virginians, who were at Centreville, closer to Manassas, also cut down trees and waited for action.

Among the three regiments closest to Manassas, Brigadier General David R. Jones' force was in place along a rail line between Manassas and the Bull Run River. Colonel Jubal Early's force covered several bridges that crossed the Bull Run. Brigadier General James Longstreet's men dug earthwork trenches around Manassas, where troops could set up guns and remain well protected from enemy fire.

Beauregard guessed that the most strategically important spot near Manassas was Henry Hill, named after Judith Henry, a woman who lived there. This high ground overlooked the best place to cross the Bull Run—a stone bridge on the Warrenton Turnpike, a wide road that ran from the northeast to the southwest. Beauregard knew his men would have to hold Henry Hill or risk losing control of four crossings on the Bull Run as well as the Warrenton Turnpike. (See map on page 13.)

Beauregard felt certain McDowell would not stage a direct attack at the stone bridge. Instead, he believed that the main Union force would cross the Bull Run at Mitchell's Ford, a mile south of the Warrenton Turnpike. Beauregard instructed Bonham to fall back from the crossroad to that position when McDowell's Union troops advanced. Cocke would then withdraw to the stone bridge, and Ewell would move his Rebel troops to Union Mill's Ford, where a railroad trestle crossed the river.

★
As soon as Union forces attacked, the Confederates planned to fall back into defensive positions.
★

11

"She took from the back of her head ...a package ... sewn up in black silk."

—Brigadier
General Bonham
describing female
Confederate spy

Beauregard reasoned that while McDowell attacked Bonham, Longstreet, Jones, and Early would lead their Rebel forces across the Bull Run and surprise McDowell by striking his left flank. Once the plan was in place, the only question was when the Federals would finally march on Manassas.

McDowell's March to Bull Run

On July 10, a young woman named Bettie Duval rode up to General Bonham's headquarters and asked to see him. She had an important message for General Beauregard, and asked Bonham to promise that it would be delivered. What happened next left the commander speechless, though he wrote about it afterward:

"[S]he took out her tucking comb and let fall the most beautiful roll of hair I have ever seen . . . . She took from the back of her head, where it was safely tied, a package not larger than a silver half dollar carefully sewn up in black silk." The package contained a message written by a source that Bonham knew to be reliable: McDowell would march on July 16.

Just as Bettie Duval's message predicted, more than 30,000 Federal troops—four divisions of about 8,000 men—left Washington on July 16. They made a colorful parade of uniforms. Though many regiments were dressed in blue, others were dressed in gray. Still others looked like French soldiers from Algeria called Zouaves, dressed in baggy red pants, blue coats, and brightly colored sashes and hats.

The march proceeded at an unusually slow pace. The majority of the Union troops were "90-day wonders" fresh from training camp. Unaccustomed to being part of a large army on the march, the men stopped to pick berries or look for water. As they neared Centreville, their progress was delayed while they cleared fallen trees left in their way by the Confederates. By the time the Federals arrived in Centreville, they had eaten all of their rations and had to wait a day for more to arrive from Washington.

With McDowell's troops delayed, Patterson and his 15,000 Union men tried to keep General Joseph E. Johnston's 11,000 Confederates near Harpers Ferry from joining up with Beauregard

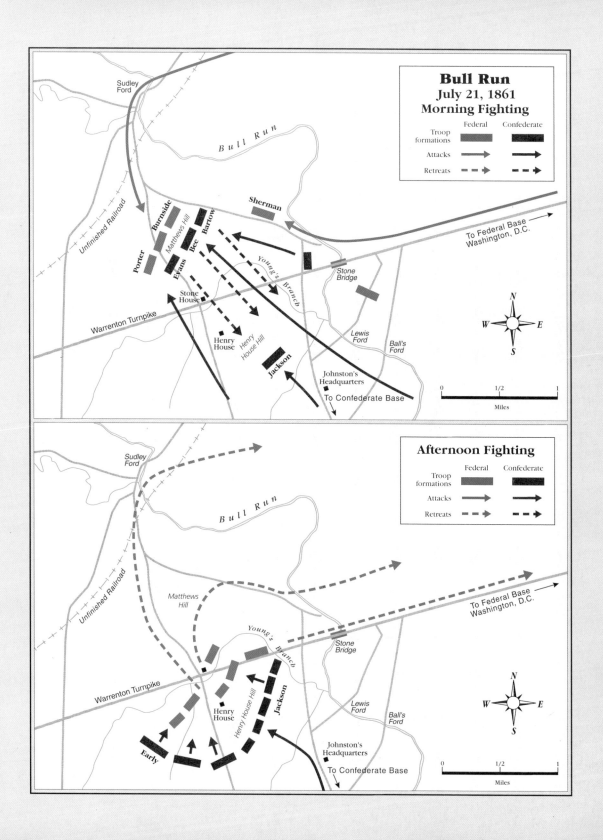

Bull Run
July 21, 1861
Morning Fighting

Troop formations — Federal / Confederate
Attacks
Retreats

Sudley Ford

Bull Run

Unfinished Railroad

Burnside

Matthews Hill

Bee

Bartow

Sherman

Porter

Evans

Young's Branch

Stone Bridge

To Federal Base
Washington, D.C.

Stone House

Warrenton Turnpike

Henry House

Henry House Hill

Lewis Ford

Ball's Ford

Jackson

Johnston's Headquarters

To Confederate Base

N
W   E
S

0   1/2   1
Miles

Afternoon Fighting

Troop formations — Federal / Confederate
Attacks
Retreats

Sudley Ford

Bull Run

Unfinished Railroad

Matthews Hill

Young's Branch

Stone Bridge

To Federal Base
Washington, D.C.

Warrenton Turnpike

Henry House

Henry House Hill

Jackson

Early

Lewis Ford

Ball's Ford

Johnston's Headquarters

To Confederate Base

N
W   E
S

0   1/2   1
Miles

A Union soldier stands guard in Centreville, about 5 miles from Manassas.

in Manassas. Patterson made no direct attacks, however, and Johnston managed to move his troops around Union lines. On July 18 and 19, the Rebels crossed the shoulder-deep waters of the Shenandoah River and boarded trains for Manassas.

In the meantime, Bonham, Cocke, and Ewell—commanders of the three Rebel regiments closest to Washington—retreated to their positions across the Bull Run. Once Johnston's men arrived, Beauregard's army would equal McDowell's in size. The delay by the Union troops in Centreville would prove very costly.

McDowell Refines His Strategy

While they were camped at Centreville, McDowell's Union scouts did reconnaissance work to determine the lay of the land and the position of the enemy troops. McDowell's scouts told him that to his left, the crossings below the stone bridge were well defended by Confederate guns. This led him to send scouts upstream where they found a lightly held crossing at Sudley Springs Ford and another closer to the bridge. McDowell decided that his First Division, under Brigadier General Daniel Tyler, would attack on the stone bridge,

Civil War Spies

The Union and the Confederacy both gained valuable information from secret agents. Bette Duval, the young woman who brought the Confederates news of McDowell's advance, worked for Rose Greenhow, a woman at the center of Washington's high society. Greenhow befriended a number of Union politicians and through her irresistible charm, extracted many secrets, that she passed along to the Confederacy. Another Rebel agent, Belle Boyd, was arrested six times for her work. Even imprisonment did not stop her; she received information from one of her contacts inside a rubber ball tossed into her prison cell window. Not all Confederate secret agents were women. Major William Norris managed a spy network that extended all the way to Montreal.

Allan Pinkerton, founder of the Secret Service, was the best known of the Union's spies. He supplied the military with information, not all of it accurate. Pinkerton and his agents were more effective at counter-spy work—identifying agents who were working for the rebels. Some of the most helpful Union spies were slaves and escaped slaves eager to help bring about a Union victory and free their comrades.

Allan Pinkerton founded the Secret Service after the war.

attempting to make the Confederates believe that this was an all-out attack when, in fact, it was a feint—a false attack designed to draw the enemy's attention away from the main thrust.

McDowell ordered the main part, Colonel D. S. Miles's Fourth Division, to remain in reserve near Centreville, and to send one brigade in another feint attack at Blackburn's Ford, well south of the stone bridge. The critical part of the plan would be carried out by the Union's Second and Third Divisions, led by Colonels David Hunter and S. P. Heintzelman. These forces would execute a turning movement against the enemy's left flank after crossing the Bull Run at Sudley's Ford. Once across, the Second and Third would sweep down the south bank of the river, freeing up the bridge and the other crossings so that the First and Fourth Divisions could bring some fresh reinforcements to the battle.

It was a good, but complicated, plan that relied on well-coordinated troop movements. Unfortunately, the work that lay ahead was difficult for young troops fresh from training. And their tasks were made even more difficult by the men and women pouring into the camps from Washington to see the battle about to take place.

The Confederate force, in the meantime, was growing larger by the hour as Johnston's men arrived by rail from Harpers Ferry. Encouraged by the growing size of his force, Beauregard decided to change his defensive plan and to attack the Federals instead. He ordered his regiments positioned below the stone bridge to cross Bull Run and crush McDowell, attacking the Union's right side.

McDowell's Early Morning Attack

In order to reach Sudley's Ford by 7 A.M. and launch an attack, McDowell's turning column—Hunter's Second and Heintzelman's Third Divisions—had to leave camp at 2 A.M. So, on Sunday, July 21, stumbling through the dark in the ruts of a cart track, the untested Union troops began a six-mile march. The two holding divisions—Tyler's First and Miles's Fourth—left an hour later.

As dawn broke, Beauregard's plans for a Rebel attack immediately fell apart. The general waited for the sound of his men's fire as they

crossed Bull Run, but the regiments below the stone bridge did not understand the timing for their advance and remained silent. A messenger arrived to report that large numbers of Union troops had been seen across Bull Run to the left of Mitchell's Ford. To prevent the Federals from crossing, Beauregard sent reserves led by Brigadier General Bernard Bee and Brigadier General Thomas Jackson to reinforce his troops in the vicinity.

The thunder of artillery and the crack of muskets soon shattered the morning calm near the stone bridge and Blackburn's Ford as Union troops feigned an attack to distract the Rebel forces. Unfortunately for McDowell, the Confederate commander at the bridge, Colonel Nathan Evans, sensed right away that the attack was a diversion.

Noticing a cloud of dust rising from the Union column on the left, Evans placed his men between Warrenton Turnpike and Matthews Hill to meet the fast-approaching first Federal regiment of Colonel Ambrose Burnside and his Rhode Islanders. Evans hid two small "twelve-pounder" cannons in a grove of trees on the hill. The cannons fired canister shot—basically tin cans filled with 70 or more musket balls packed in sawdust—that made the guns into giant shotguns. The artillery had a clear line of fire to the open road. Shortly after 9 A.M., the Rebels spotted Burnside's troops and fired.

Suddenly the air was thick with whistling canister shot and whizzing bullets. Hunter, the commander of McDowell's Second

Colonel Burnside's Rhode Island troops attacked Confederate positions and came under intense fire.

★

Fighting began shortly after 9 A.M. Rebel troops met Federals between Sudley Ford and the Warrenton Turnpike at Matthews Hill.

★

17

The Union Commanders

Winfield Scott

Born in Virginia in 1786, Winfield Scott never considered leaving the U.S. Army for the Confederacy. As general-in-chief of the Union army, Scott was responsible for overall military strategy. His plan for bringing the South to its knees by cutting off crucial supplies, however, was not aggressive enough for an impatient public. People could not understand why this bold hero of the Mexican War (1846–1848), was not more eager to attack. Some even thought he was soft on Virginia.

Scott was seventy-four and nicknamed "Old Fuss and Feathers." He had had a long military career and he had also run unsuccessfully for president in 1852 against Franklin Pierce. Although Scott suffered from the effects of old age and poor health, he remained sharp and well in control of the Union's military operations. A few months after Bull Run, in November 1861, Scott retired from the army. He died in 1866.

Irvin McDowell commanded Union forces at Bull Run.

Irvin McDowell

General Irvin McDowell had a reputation for efficiency. He was also known for his sharp tongue and enormous appetite—both of which made him unpopular with some of his men.

After the Union lost at Bull Run, McDowell was replaced by George B. McClellan, who put him in charge of a division.

William T. Sherman, who fought at Bull Run, thought McDowell was blamed unfairly for the Union loss, declaring that McDowell had created "one of the best planned battles of the war."

At the Second Battle of Bull Run in 1862, McDowell was again assigned some of the blame for defeat, and was removed from his command. He died in 1885 at the age of 67.

William Tecumseh Sherman

William Tecumseh Sherman was an unknown forty-one-year-old colonel from Ohio when he fought at the battle of Manassas. Although he fought in General Daniel Tyler's First Division with exceptional courage, he took the defeat badly. Three days later he wrote, "I am sufficiently disgraced now. I suppose I can sneak into some quiet corner." Instead, however, he went on to become one of the greatest generals in U.S. history.

William T. Sherman proved to be one of the Union's most valuable commanders.

When Ulysses S. Grant became commander-in-chief of the army, Sherman took his place as supreme commander in the West. By then, he was a brigadier general. He was largely responsible for the fall of Atlanta in September 1864. Sherman believed it would be impossible for the North to win unless the fighting spirit of the South was broken. Lincoln agreed. In November, Sherman began his famous "march to the sea" through Georgia with 600,000 Federals under his command. Then he advanced through South Carolina, burning every building in sight and leaving a trail of ruin 60 miles wide behind him.

After the war, Sherman was promoted to general and succeeded Ulysses S. Grant as commander of the U.S. Army. He died in 1891.

★

Rebel reinforce-
ments arrived at
10 A.M. by rail.

★

Brigade, was soon struck. "I leave the matter in your hands," he said to Burnside, blood dripping down his neck.

Burnside's entire force soon came under intense fire, as did Colonel Andrew Porter's, also in the Second Division. When they fell back for a moment, Evans ordered the Confederate First Louisiana Battalion, led by Major Roberdeau Wheat, into action. Wheat's men charged, waving their glistening razor-sharp Bowie knives and yelling in unison. The unearthly sounds of the Confederates added to the Federals' confusion and fear. It was the first of many battles in which the "Rebel Yell" announced a charging wave of Confederates.

"Wheat's Tigers" managed to stop the advance of the growing number of Federals for a while, though many "Tigers" were killed in the process, and Wheat himself was badly injured. Carried to the field surgeons at the back of the line and told that he would not live, Wheat replied, "I don't feel like dying yet." True to his word, he lived another year before he was killed in battle.

Evans feared his Confederate line would not hold much longer. At about 10 A.M. he got word that Bee's Rebel brigade was arriving by rail lines to his rear. Bee led his men to the action west of Matthew's

By noon, Union and Confederate troops were in full battle.

Hill. Before he headed out, however, he instructed the commander of his artillery, Captain John Imboden, to place his big guns in front of the farmhouse on Henry Hill. "Here is the battlefield," he said to Imboden. "And we are in for it!"

Behind Bee came Colonel Francis Bartow, whose Confederate troops had also taken the train from the Harpers Ferry region. He placed his men on Bee's right at the crest of Matthews Hill.

Even with these fresh reinforcements, the Rebels were outnumbered. By late morning, the Federals had pushed the Rebels across Warrenton Turnpike and up the slopes of Henry Hill. Some Confederate regiments began to retreat, and it looked as if McDowell would celebrate a great victory. The good news reached the Union supporters about two miles away who had come to watch the action. They had been unable to see anything through the thick smoke of battle.

Evans, Bee, and Bartow had suffered serious losses, but Beauregard was by no means ready to give up. He ordered Cocke and Early to move their troops to Henry Hill, where Jackson was already in place. The Confederate commander realized that, with the hill under his control, McDowell's Federals would have to fight their way around or over the high ground to cut off the Rebels from Richmond.

"Standing Like a Stone Wall!"

At about 11:30 A.M., with the battle still raging around Matthews Hill, Jackson ordered Imboden's artillery battery and one of his own to dig into a position at the top of Henry Hill. Then he placed his regiments around them and ordered them to lie low beneath the crest of the hill. From there, his well-trained troops could hold a strong defensive position.

Meanwhile, in the flat fields below, Bee's troops were falling back under a hail of gunfire from the Federals. Bee knew he had to rally his men before an orderly retreat turned into panic and led to even greater losses. Pointing up the hill toward Jackson he cried above

'Rally around the Virginians!'
—General Bernard Bee

21

The Southern Commanders

Pierre G. T. Beauregard

Historians agree that Beauregard

was more talented as a military engineer than as a field commander. Born to a wealthy family in Louisiana in 1818, he looked as if he was born to command.

Pierre Beauregard commanded the Confederate Army.

Although he was not tall, he walked with an erect, military posture and was a handsome man. The Battle of Bull Run was one of the brightest moments in his military career.

Beauregard graduated second in his class from West Point—his future enemy, Irvin McDowell, was twenty-third in the same class. He served as an engineer on Winfield Scott's staff during the Mexican War, helping him capture Mexico City. When the Confederacy was formed, Beauregard was given a command at Charleston, South Carolina, where he managed to win Fort Sumter from the Union without losing one man. After Bull Run, he retired from the army because of poor health. He returned to defend the coasts of Georgia and South Carolina against Union attack in 1863. After the war, he was a railroad president and then a manager of Louisiana's state lottery. He died in 1893.

Thomas J. "Stonewall" Jackson

Thomas Jackson had been a professor at the Virginia Military Institute for ten years when the Civil

"Stonewall" Jackson was a brilliant strategist for the South.

War began. His stern and humorless personality did not make him a very popular teacher, but he was an inspired commander.

Jackson's guiding strategic rule was "always mystify, mislead, and surprise the enemy." After Bull Run, he put this rule into action in his brilliant Shenandoah Valley Campaign in 1862, when he helped prevent McClellan and huge Union armies massed outside of Richmond, Virginia, from attacking the city.

The following May, he led 30,000 men on a daylong march that ended in a surprise attack on the Union army in Chancellorsville, Virginia. It was a smashing victory for the Rebels. During that battle, Jackson was accidentally shot by his men. He died ten days later at age 39.

Joseph E. Johnston

Joseph E. Johnston was a Virginian to the core, but he devoted much of his life to the Union after graduation from West Point. Johnston was wounded five times in the Mexican War while under the command of Winfield Scott. Twelve years later, in 1860, he became the quarter-master-general of the U.S. Army. In the spring of 1861, when he tearfully told Secretary of War Simon Cameron that

Joseph Johnston was a gifted defensive commander.

he was joining the Confederacy, he expressed his great affection for the Union. "I owe all that I am to the government of the United States," he said. "It has educated me and clothed me with honor."

Johnston was a cautious fighter and a gifted defensive commander. He managed to obstruct William Tecumseh Sherman's march through North Carolina at the close of the Civil War. After the war, he served in the House of Representatives and later became the commissioner of railroads. Johnston grew to be a good friend of General William Sherman, his old enemy. He died five weeks after Sherman, at the age of eighty-four.

The troops of Bee, Bartow, and Evans rallied behind "Stonewall" Jackson at Henry Hill.

★

By 1 P.M. Federal forces had crossed the Bull Run. They attacked the Rebels at Henry Hill.

★

the gunfire, "There is Jackson standing like a stone wall. Rally around the Virginians!" This battle cry gave the legendary Confederate leader his unforgettable nickname: "Stonewall" Jackson. Bee died soon afterward, riding into enemy fire at the head of his troops.

By early afternoon, Heintzelman's division of Federals had joined Hunter's in the attack. Tyler's division came pouring across the stone bridge. Among those troops was a brigade led by Colonel William Tecumseh Sherman, a man whose name would be well known by the war's end. Firing as they charged, with battle flags raised, the Federals streamed up Henry Hill, where Jackson and his men stood ready with their muskets loaded and cannons primed. Suddenly, the Virginians fired into the Federals at close range. One volley after another struck the Federals, bodies fell on top of bodies. The survivors stumbled back down the slope of the hill, where they were ordered to re-form their ranks and charge again. The hunger for the fight, however, had left the Federals, and the new charge was only half-hearted.

Bull Run/Manassas

By this time, Beauregard had joined the Rebel fighters, riding along the battle line to spur them on. Johnston, in the meantime, had set up a command post at a road intersection and rushed reinforcements to Henry Hill.

The two sides were now about equal in number. While the Rebel line had grown due to a constant stream of reinforcements coming in by rail, McDowell had been unable to get his two reserve Union brigades into action. Even worse, many of his soldiers at the front were exhausted, having marched and fought for fourteen hours in Virginia's blistering summer heat.

The Federals Run

By late afternoon, Beauregard realized his advantage and ordered a counterattack. The entire line of Rebels surged forward, yelling, as Jackson had instructed them earlier, "like furies." Seeing the counterattack advancing downhill at them, Federal troops turned and began running past their officers on horseback, who screamed

The ruins of Henry House after the battle.

for them to stand. As the whooping Rebels continued their advance, Federal soldiers threw away guns and packs, scrambling wildly back across Bull Run.

McDowell tried to prevent a bad situation from becoming a disaster. He sent two brigades, who had been at the fords below the stone bridge, and some fresh troops to form a line near Centreville. He hoped that the men retreating from Henry Hill would join their comrades and help them stop the Rebels' counterattack. Instead, the growing panic of the retreating Federals spread into mass hysteria, scattering even the fresh troops, and threatening civilians who could not move out the way fast enough.

Some congressmen tried to stop the soldiers, who seemed determined to run all the way to Washington in what later became known as the "great skedaddle." But the panic spread. The dignitaries and socialites who had come to Manassas on a "summer excursion" got more than they bargained for. Instead of entertainment, they saw gruesome bloodshed and death.

Not every unit had run. Some in Sherman's brigade, in particular, stood firm, forming a rear guard to slow the Rebels. The triumphant Confederates chased the Union troops only a mile or two past Bull

Union attacks were stopped by Confederate counterattacks.

Run. Then they turned their attention to celebrating their victory and dealing with the hundreds of Union prisoners they had captured.

President Jefferson Davis arrived on the battlefield just as the Confederates realized victory was theirs. On the field, he urged the Rebels to continue pursuit of the Federals. The daylong battle, however, had exhausted his troops. To make matters worse, a heavy rain began that night and continued the next day, turning roads into mud.

Union wounded wait at a field hospital.

After Bull Run

Compared with other battles of the Civil War, the number of dead and wounded at Bull Run do not qualify it as one of the bloodiest battles of the war. The North lost about 3,000 men who were dead or wounded. The South suffered about 1,200 casualties. There were several aspects of the Battle of Bull Run, however, that made it extremely significant.

In the South, confidence in the superior ability of Rebel troops and generals grew as word of the victory at Manassas spread. The Rebels had beaten an army almost twice their size. Southerners expressed pride, as well as scorn for their enemy. *The Mobile Register* crowed that the Federals would "never again advance beyond cannon shot of Washington."

The mood in the North was understandably gloomy after Bull Run. Horace Greeley, whose New York *Herald Tribune* had contributed to the fever that led to the battle, even suggested that Lincoln make peace with the Confederacy.

President Lincoln was upset by the loss, but determined to preserve the Union.

The First Modern War

The Civil War has sometimes been called "the first modern war" because it was the first major conflict in which ironclad, steam-powered ships engaged in battle. It was also the first war in which railroads were used to carry supplies and troops into battle. In fact, it was the arrival of

Advances in artillery gave the big guns greater range and accuracy.

Confederate reinforcements from Harpers Ferry by rail that helped Rebel forces win the Battle of Bull Run.

The main aspect of the Civil War that brought it into the modern era, however, were the weapons used.

Throughout the 1700s and 1800s, the accepted battle strategy was to march massed troops into attack—in close formation—across open fields. Civil War soldiers marched into battle separated by no more than a foot on all sides. Before the Civil War, a soldier might get off one or two shots from his musket before reaching enemy lines. Attackers and defenders would then use their guns as clubs or stab at each other with bayonets attached to the gun barrel.

By the early 1860s, however, modern gun makers had developed the technique of rifling their weapons. Grooves were cut into the gun barrel that caused the bullet to spin as it was fired. That spin added distance and accuracy to a rifle shot. In the American Revolution, muskets were not accurate beyond 100 yards. Civil War muskets were accurate at more than 800 yards.

Firing mechanisms had also advanced by the Civil War. Muskets used an explosive mercury charge instead of an unpredictable flint firing piece to fire the bullet, which cut down on misfires and made the guns more reliable. Civil War guns fired cone-shaped projectiles called minié balls. These bullets were made of soft lead and shattered into many pieces when they struck, causing gaping wounds.

As the war dragged on, rifles became even more deadly, with greater range and accuracy. Toward the end of the war, Union troops were supplied with breech-, or top-, loading weapons to replace the slower muzzle-, or front-, loading models. This meant that Union troops could fire more than a dozen shots in a minute, compared to the three shots per minute a well-trained soldier could fire from a front-loading gun.

Considering these advances, it is obvious that charges across open areas would lead to enormous losses. Closely packed ranks of soldiers were mowed down like wheat. Sadly, as modern as the Civil War may have been, the advances in technologies only brought more horror and death than had previously been possible.

Steam-powered gunboats were the first modern ships to fight in a war.

Union troops leaving the battle area.

In the long run, however, the loss at Bull Run was actually good for the Federals, and the victory was bad for the Confederacy. Many historians believe that the South's triumph in the first battle of the Civil War made it difficult for them to prepare for all the fighting that would follow. Mary Boykin Chestnut, the wife of one of Beauregard's aides, expressed her frustration in the diary she kept throughout the war: "Here we will dillydally . . . until they get up an army three times as large as McDowell's that we have just defeated . . . . This victory . . . lulls us into a fool's paradise of conceit."

Northerners, who realized that the war would not be won quickly or easily, became more determined to beat the Rebels. They also became better organized. Mary Chestnut's observations were correct: Lincoln immediately called for 1,000,000 additional troops. He also replaced McDowell with a new commander of the Union troops in Washington.

It was many months before the Federals and the Confederates met again in a major battle. Those on both sides, who had hoped that Bull Run would be the war's decisive battle, soon learned that a great deal more blood would have to be spilled before the Civil War would actually end.

★ ★ ★

"This victory . . . lulls us into a fool's paradise."
—*Mary Chestnut*

★ ★ ★

Glossary

artillery large weapons used by fighting forces that fall into three categories—guns or cannons, howitzers, and mortars

brigade a military unit smaller than a division, usually consisting of three to five regiments of 500 to 1,000 soldiers

commander a military leader, usually holding the rank of general

corps a military grouping of between 10,000 and 20,000 soldiers

division a military grouping of between 6,000 and 8,000 soldiers or two to three brigades

feint in military usage, an attack on one part of the enemy's line in order to distract attention from the main point of attack

ford a crossing on a stream or river.

quartermaster officer in charge of providing food, clothing, shelter, and other basic supplies

regiment a military unit smaller than a brigade and a division. In the Civil War soldiers fought in the same regiment throughout the war with fellow soldiers who were usually from the same state, city, or town

reinforce in military terms, to strengthen a military unit by sending in fresh troops.

For More Information

Books

Brooks, Victor. *Secret Weapons in the Civil War* (Untold History of the Civil War). New York: Chelsea, 1999,

Fleischman, Paul. *Bull Run*. New York: HarperCollins, 1999.

Smith, C. Carter. *The First Battles: A Sourcebook on the Civil War* (American Albums from the Collections of the Library of Congress). Brookfield, CT: Millbrook Press, 2000.

Wilbur, Keith C. *Civil War Medicine* 1861-1865 (Living History). New York: Chelsea House, 1999.

Web Sites

The Battle of Bull Run
   Learn more about the Battle of Bull Run and the soldiers who fought—
   www.civilwarhome.com/1manassa.htm
Manassas National Battlefield Park
   Find out more information about and see pictures of the battlefield at Bull Run—
   www.nps.gov/mana/home.htm

Index

"Anaconda Plan," 8
Antietam, 4, 9

Bartow, Francis, 21
Battle names, 9
Beauregard, Pierre, 8,
    10, 12, 14–17,
    22–23, 25, 27
Bee, Bernard, 17,
    20–21
Blackburn's Ford,
    16–17
Bonham, Milledge, 10,
    12, 14–15
Boyd, Belle, 13
Bull Run River, 6, 11
Burnside, Ambrose, 17

Cameron, Simon, 24
Centreville, 12–15, 26
Chestnut, Mary
    Boykin, 27, 30
Cocke, Philip St.
    George, 12, 15, 21
Cotton, 4

Davis, Jefferson, 8, 27
Duval, Bettie, 13–14

Early, Jubal, 12, 21
Evans, Nathan, 17,
    20–21
Ewell, Richard, 12, 15

Fort Sumter, 5, 8, 23

Gettysburg, 4

Grant, Ulysses S., 19
Greeley, Horace, 27
Greenhow, Rose, 13
Gunboats, 8, 29

Harpers Ferry, 10, 14,
    16, 21, 28
Heintzelman, 16, 22
Henry, Judith, 12
Henry Hill, 12, 21–22,
    26
Hunter, David, 16–17,
    22

Imboden, John, 20–21

Jackson, Thomas, 17,
    21–25
Johnston, Joseph E.,
    14–16, 22, 24
Jones, David, 12

Kansas-Nebraska Act, 5

Lincoln, Abraham, 5,
    10, 27, 30
Longstreet, James, 12

Matthews Hill, 17,
    20–21
McClellan, George, 18,
    24
McDowell, Irvin, 10,
    12–19, 21, 23,
    25–26, 30
Missouri Compromise,
    5

Miles, D.S., 15–16
Mill's Ford, 12
Mitchell's Ford, 12, 16
Modern War, 28–29

Norris, William, 13

Patterson, Robert, 10,
    14
Pierce, Franklin, 18
Picnic, 6
Pinkerton, Allan, 13
Pittsburg Landing, 9
Porter, Andrew, 17

Rhode Islanders, 17

Scott, Winfield, 8, 10,
    18, 23–24
Sharpsburg, 9
Sherman, William, 19,
    22, 24, 26
Shiloh, 9
Slaves, 4–5, 13
Spies, 13
Sudley Springs Ford,
    15–16

Tyler, Daniel, 15–16,
    19, 22

Warrentown Turnpike,
    12, 17, 21
West Point, 10, 23–24
Wheat, Roberdeau, 20

Zouaves, 14